The Goldman Project

by Staci Swedeen

A SAMUEL FRENCH ACTING EDITION

SAMUEL FRENCH

FOUNDED 1830

NEW YORK HOLLYWOOD LONDON TORONTO

SAMUELFRENCH.COM

IMPORTANT BILLING AND CREDIT
REQUIREMENTS

THE GOLDMAN PROJECT was originally presented by the Penguin Repertory Company with Joe Brancato, artistic director and Andrew M. Horn, executive director, in October 2006. It was directed by Joe Brancato with sets by James Dardenne, costumes by Patricia E. Doherty, lighting design by Jeffery Nellis, and sound design by Dimitri Tisseyre. The production stage manager was Jack D. McDowell. The cast was as follows:

TONY MARKS . . . . Sam Guncler
AVIVA LEVINE . . . . Bernadette Quigley
NAOMI GOLDMAN . . . . Anita Keal

THE GOLDMAN PROJECT was presented in an Off Broadway co-production by the Abingdon Theatre Company (Jan Buttram, artistic director, Samuel J. Bellinger, managing director, and Kim T. Sharp, associate artistic director) and the Penguin Repertory Company in October 2007. It was directed by Joe Brancato with sets by Ken Larson, costumes by Patricia E. Doherty, lighting design by Matthew McCarthy, and sound design by Dimitri Tisseyre. The production manager was Ian Grunes. The production stage manager was Jack D. McDowell. The cast was as follows:

TONY MARKS . . . . Sam Guncler
AVIVA LEVINE . . . . Bernadette Quigley
NAOMI GOLDMAN . . . . Anita Keal

A New York State Council for the Arts grant assisted in the early writing of this play.

CHARACTERS

(in order of appearance)

TONY MARKS - Naomi's adult son, a singer.

AVIVA LEVINE - Tony's college girlfriend, an artist.

NAOMI GOLDMAN - Mother of Tony, widow, survivor of Auschwitz. She speaks with a pronounced Rumanian (Hungarian) accent. Well dressed, wears a wig.

TIME

1994

PLACE

Naomi Goldman's small apartment near 186th Street in the Inwood section of upper Manhattan. An entry hall leads to the small but comfortable living room. Off the living room is an exit to the kitchen. Another exit to a hallway and bedrooms. There are bookshelves, a television set and photos on many surfaces. It has the look of an elderly woman's apartment. There are also numerous boxes scattered about containing items Naomi has been ordering from shopping shows.

AUTHOR'S NOTES

The inspiration for *The Goldman Project* came from meeting Gertie Wurtzburger, a spunky, vivacious Rumanian woman I first encountered when my husband and I purchased a cabin in the Catskills. In 2003 I interviewed her about her experiences during World War II. Portions of her testimony have been incorporated into this play.

But a playwright's job is to imagine, explore, question, and consider. While *The Goldman Project* is a work of fiction, it delves into real issues of family, loss, guilt and the poisonous nature of secrets kept silent.

Elie Wiesel said that "I have learned two lessons in my life: first, there are no sufficient literary, psychological or historical answers to human tragedy, only moral ones. Second, just as despair can come to one another only from other human beings, hope, too, can be given to one only by other human beings."

Many people have offered me hope and support in the journey of this play. Thanks to Joe Brancato and Andrew Horn of Penguin Repertory Theatre, the Abingdon Theatre Company and the generosity of my original cast and crew. I also want to thank Arthur and Madelaine Warren, Mara Mills, Luly Kaufman, and my husband Chris Skelly.

This play is dedicated to Florence Swedeen and Gertie Wurtzburger with love and respect.

Scene One

(The sound of a television blaring away. Lights up. Sound of keys, a door opening and closing. **TONY** *and* **AVIVA** *enter.* **TONY** *puts his gym bag in the corner and calls out over the television.)*

TELEVISION NEWSCASTER. Richard M. Nixon died last night at Cornell Medical Center after slipping into a coma. President Clinton has declared a national day of mourning. Meanwhile, in the mass tribal killings in Rwanda, the International Red Cross estimates that tens, perhaps hundreds, or thousands of people, mainly Tutsis, have been massacred. When asked if this is a genocide, State Department spokeswoman Christine Shelley had this to say –

TONY. *(overlapping over the announcer until he turns off the television.)* Ma!? Ma?!!

(He briefly looks in the other rooms, returns.)

TONY. Guess she's not here. You wanna wait or…?

AVIVA. Sure.

TONY. So?

AVIVA. So…I was nervous about contacting you.

TONY. I don't remember you ever being nervous – about anything.

AVIVA. I still owe you an apology.

TONY. For what?

AVIVA. The way I broke up with you.

TONY. Water over the dam.

AVIVA. Under the bridge.

TONY. Whatever.

AVIVA. Not that any of that matters now.

TONY. No. Ancient history.

AVIVA. Right.

(Pause. They both laugh nervously. AVIVA *looks around the apartment)*

Oh my god.

TONY. What? What?!

AVIVA. This apartment is like a time capsule. Everything looks just the way it did when we were – you know –

TONY. Younger?

AVIVA. Yeah.

(looking around)

How long have your folks lived here now?

TONY. Forever. My mother's never going to leave. They'll have to carry her out in her sequins and heels.

AVIVA. I remember she loved to get dressed up.

TONY. Wholesale. My father was in the business.

AVIVA. That's right, that's right. So he's retired now…?

TONY. As retired as you can get.

AVIVA. *(off his expression)* Oh god, Tony –

TONY. Heart attack.

AVIVA. I'm sorry.

TONY. Almost a year ago. But I don't want to talk about him; I want to talk about you – and what you're doing here. I mean, here you are, in the flesh –

AVIVA. A little more flesh than when you knew me.

TONY. You look good.

AVIVA. Liar.

TONY. I mean it. You do.

AVIVA. Thanks.

TONY. I wondered if you'd, I don't know, moved out of New York.

AVIVA. Yeah, I did.

TONY. You moved? You're kidding. Where?

AVIVA. New Jersey. And don't make a joke about it.

TONY. You said you'd *never* leave the city.

AVIVA. Life can take us to some pretty unexpected places, huh?

TONY. Speaking of the unexpected – how'd you find me, anyway?

AVIVA. Ever hear of a phone book?

TONY. The concept sounds familiar.

AVIVA. Actually, I was looking to see if your parents still lived at the same address. I thought about contacting them without contacting you –

TONY. You *did*? I would have felt –

AVIVA. I know, I know…I *wanted* to know how you are but –

TONY. But what?

AVIVA. I'm glad your wife gave you the message. She sounded very nice.

TONY. She does. She can be, sometimes. Nice.

AVIVA. I was really glad you called me back. I wasn't sure if you would.

TONY. Of course I'd call you back. I mean, you want a picture, right?

AVIVA. Yes, well, it's a *little* more complicated than that.

TONY. Intriguing. Can I get you something to drink?

AVIVA. Water would be great. Thanks.

(**TONY** *exits to the kitchen.*)

AVIVA. Oh look! I always loved this picture of you from your bar mitzvah!

TONY. You break it, you buy it.

AVIVA. No sale! Look at you! That hair!

TONY. (*re-entering with glass of water*) I was a style prodigy.

AVIVA. And those clothes!

TONY. Wholesale, remember. Here's your water.

AVIVA. Thanks. God! Everything looks exactly just the way I remember it.

TONY. Do you remember this couch?

AVIVA. Sure.

TONY. No – I mean do you "*remember*" this couch, one very special night on this – ?

(*There is the sound of a door opening.*)

NAOMI. Hello? Is someone here?

TONY. Ma! It's me!

NAOMI. Me who?

TONY. *(calling out loudly)* Me who do you think?

NAOMI. Tony, is that you?

TONY. Yes, Ma. With company.

NAOMI. Company?

TONY. *(to* **AVIVA***)* I keep trying to get her to wear her damn hearing aid. I have to yell and repeat things. She can really drive me crazy.

(**NAOMI** *enters. She is a small, energetic older woman. She wears a stylish wig and dresses very well. She is carrying a recent purchase.*)

Ma, do you remember Aviva? My, uh – friend – from college?

NAOMI. Aviva! Of course I remember Aviva!

(a pause as she looks at **AVIVA***)*

Is *this* Aviva? She looks different.

AVIVA. I'm older.

NAOMI. You don't know from old.

AVIVA. Don't you remember – Tony used to bring me here for dinner?

NAOMI. Aviva! I remember now. I once made you my stuffed chicken with the whole skin and the vings. Oh! Elaine tells me I shouldn't say vings. I should say "wings."

AVIVA. Elaine.

NAOMI. My daughter-in-law Elaine. You're Jewish, right?

AVIVA. Yes.

NAOMI. *(to* **TONY***)* Elaine isn't. *(to* **AVIVA***)* You know her?

TONY. Ma, come on. They never met *(muttering)* and probably never will.

NAOMI. Vat did you say?

TONY. What's in the package?

NAOMI. Nothing, Mr. Snoopy.

TONY. *(to* AVIVA*)* My mother buys so much stuff from QVC that the UPS man thinks she's sick if he doesn't stop by here everyday.

NAOMI. What else should I do with my money? Spend it on my grandchildren?

TONY. Ouch.

NAOMI. Have you eaten? Are you hungry?

TONY. We just got here.

NAOMI. Let me put on some coffee, then. Maybe a few sandwiches…

(She exits to the kitchen.)

AVIVA. She looks great.

TONY. Hear that, Ma? You look great!

NAOMI. *(from off)* What?

TONY. *(loudly for* NAOMI*'s benefit)* You're gonna live to be a hundred.

NAOMI. *(from off)* Who wants to live to be a hundred?

TONY. *(to* AVIVA*)* She's like that energizer bunny. Just keeps going. Mahjong, JCC, tenants association and listening to the news – at full volume.

AVIVA. She really looks good.

TONY. Well, since Dad died her blood pressure's gone through the roof, and she sees the Doctor for a few other ailments, but otherwise…So how is *your* mother? Still okay?

*(*AVIVA *makes a face.)*

Oh, god. I'm sorry. Did your mother die?

AVIVA. No. But I may have to kill her.

TONY. *(laughing)* I remember you two were always going at it.

AVIVA. I'm glad you find it so amusing.

*(*TONY *looks at her fondly.)*

What are you looking at?

TONY. You. If someone would have said to me that I'd be standing in this apartment with you after all these years –

AVIVA. Well, after you got married it didn't seem very appropriate to stay in touch.

TONY. When was the last time *you* worried about appropriate?

AVIVA. What do you mean?!

TONY. I'll never forget that photo exhibition you did in college – and once people actually figured out what they were looking at –

AVIVA. Orifices –

TONY. Orifices…assholes! Man! That was some show.

AVIVA. *(laughing)* And weren't some of the pictures of your ass?

TONY. *(overlapping)* The best ones! Didn't you get a grant for that, some big fellowship?

AVIVA. Yeah.

TONY. Are you still involved with all that arty stuff?

AVIVA. Yeah – though I'm branching out in some other areas.

TONY. *(Bogart impression)* "Of all the gin joints in all the world." You know, I've thought of you over the years. Often.

So what are you doing now?

(NAOMI enters with a tray piled with food.)

AVIVA. How lovely, Mrs. Goldman! Did you just throw that together?

NAOMI. I was remembering you, Aviva – when Tony would bring you here for dinner. You were very passionate, very political. A regular socialist.

AVIVA. Yes, I guess you could say that.

NAOMI. Are you still saving the world?

AVIVA. Trying.

NAOMI. Good.

AVIVA. It seems to keep getting into trouble.

TONY. At least there was some good news recently. Nixon died.

AVIVA. Aren't you curious to hear what's on those hours of secret tapes? Can you even imagine?

NAOMI. Aviva, you're not eating. You don't like?

AVIVA. *(dutifully taking a sandwich)* Oh, thank you. Anyway, I'm currently working on this project, Mrs. Goldman –

NAOMI. What did you say?

AVIVA. *(louder)* A new project I'm working on –

NAOMI. *(to* TONY*)* See, she doesn't mumble, I can *hear her.*

(to AVIVA*)*

Tony got me a hearing aid last month. What do I need a hearing aid for?

TONY. Are you serious?!

NAOMI. Thirteen hundred dollars. He says I need it because he has to repeat himself.

TONY. Mother! You don't hear half of what I say!

NAOMI. Besides, who has to hear everything? I can't hear so good, I can't see so good, I'm old.

AVIVA. You're not old.

NAOMI. Then I'm *young* and I don't see or hear so good.

TONY. Fine. You're ancient.

NAOMI. I am not! I get out, I go, I do. Was I here when you came? No. I go to the store. I go shopping. *(to* AVIVA*)* For Rosh Hashana, I went to my synagogue 'cause I bought a ticket and went.

TONY. How much are they charging now?

NAOMI. Why, you wanted to come?

TONY. No, I want to know what's the going rate for prayer.

NAOMI. 125 dollars a ticket, 25 for a donation.

TONY. So 150?

NAOMI. I gave an extra 25 to say a prayer for your father.

TONY. *(under his breath)* Man. That's some racket.

NAOMI. It's not a racket, it's synagogue.

TONY. How come every time I *don't* want you to hear me you do?

NAOMI. So I shouldn't say a prayer for your father?

TONY. I didn't say that.

NAOMI. Say what?

AVIVA. I'm so sorry to hear about your husband, Mrs. Goldman.

NAOMI. I married the best man in the whole world. Every night he brought me flowers. We lived together for 49 years like honeymooners. *(to* **TONY***)* Your father was a wonderful guy. I had a special life with him.

TONY. *(overlapping)* How can you say that!

NAOMI. Say what?

TONY. I mean, talk about someone who could be a *real* asshole.

NAOMI. Derkheritz! *("Respect!")* Now that he's dead you say these things?

TONY. There was certainly no talking to him while he was alive.

NAOMI. Drey mire nisht meyn kop! *("Don't make me crazy.")*

TONY. Du dreyst meyn kop! The way you are always standing up for him. Farvos makhst im oys gut? *("Why do you make him out to be good?")*

NAOMI. He was good to me.

TONY. Okay, okay.

NAOMI. And he was better to you than you'll ever know!

TONY. Let's drop it.

NAOMI. He was there for you when –

TONY. Let's drop it! Let's talk about how altruistic the synagogue is and why you have to fork over money to walk in the door.

NAOMI. I am more fortunate than many. Without donations how else can the doors stay open? So I pay.

TONY. *(to* **AVIVA***)* There goes my inheritance.

NAOMI. What inheritance?

(to **AVIVA***)*

See! There's nothing wrong with my hearing.

AVIVA. Mrs. Goldman, this project that I'm working on, it's kind of a big deal. Really big.

NAOMI. What?

TONY. *(loudly)* Aviva's visiting today because she's – because why?

AVIVA. It's pretty straightforward, actually. I'm doing these interviews with a camcorder –

TONY. Oh, you're taking camcorders into orifices now? You've become a proctologist?!

NAOMI. You're a doctor?

AVIVA. No, no, I'm not a doctor.

TONY. With you, I figure it *has* to be something interesting. What are you poking into now? Is this a subject you can mention in front of my mother?

NAOMI. I don't know what the two of you are talking about. What subject? What poking?

AVIVA. It's a subject your mother really knows something about.

TONY. Stuffed chicken?

AVIVA. The war.

NAOMI. Yes, I see, every night on the TV there is a war…

AVIVA. No, I mean World War II.

TONY. *(overlapping)* Aviva.

AVIVA. I'm involved with a project on the Shoah, Mrs. Goldman.

TONY. Aviva!

AVIVA. I've been interviewing survivors. When I was doing some research at the Holocaust Museum –

TONY. Oh, great.

AVIVA. This was started by Steven Speilberg? Schindler's List?

NAOMI. I haven't seen.

AVIVA. It's very…(powerful.)

NAOMI. I heard. He made I.T.

TONY. E.T., Mother, not I.T.

NAOMI. Okay. It was cute.

AVIVA. Yes, but this isn't that. While making the film Schindler's List, he was inspired to start this foundation. We're taping oral and visual histories which will be archived so that these stories are preserved. We're racing against the clock because it won't be long before everyone is…I mean, these stories will be lost. No one will know what so many people – like you – went through.

(NAOMI exits down the hall.)

Oh shit.

TONY. *This* is why you called me after all these years?

AVIVA. Not the only reason, but –

TONY. Are you nuts?

AVIVA. I didn't lead into it the right way. I wanted to spend a little time together first, talk about other things, catch up with you and – I didn't set this up correctly.

(going towards the hallway, calling out)

Mrs. Goldman? Mrs. Goldman?

TONY. Could it be more obvious? She doesn't *want* to talk about it.

AVIVA. Let me apologize, see if –

TONY. Leave her alone.

AVIVA. Tony – come on. Once she understands –

TONY. Understands what?

AVIVA. How important this is! That there is this narrow window of opportunity to –

TONY. You know, you've got real balls.

AVIVA. Ovaries – and listen –

TONY. I mean, for you, this subject is at a nice distance.

AVIVA. Meaning?

TONY. Were *your* parents in the camps?

AVIVA. You know they weren't, but –

TONY. There's no "but" about it. You don't get it and you won't ever really get it so what's the point of going on about it? Just to keep making everyone feel bad?

AVIVA. Tony, when I used to ask you *anything* about your parents you always deflected, told a joke, said it was no big deal but it was obvious that –

TONY. What? That I was fucked up?

AVIVA. I didn't say that.

TONY. You know how I survived this family? By not getting sucked into that Holocaust shit. Not everyone feels the need to go around talking about it. My father didn't want to talk about it. If it came up, he'd leave the room – like she just did.

AVIVA. I remember your father as a very sweet man, very old world and protective of your mother.

TONY. He was a control freak…

AVIVA. And you're still mad at him, aren't you?

TONY. Look, Freud, when you've straightened out things in your own family, then you can talk.
When I was five she made some kind of a casserole with onions. I hated onions! I refused to eat it. It was like World War III. I locked myself in the bathroom. He busted the door down. But he never hit me so she had to get the belt out and she beat the crap out of me "for not listening to him and to learn a lesson to respect the meal." Here's the lesson I learned – lay low, keep out of their way and never expect that anything I ever do would be good enough.

AVIVA. How often did things like that happen?

TONY. Change the subject.

AVIVA. Okay. Here's why I think it's so critical your mother tell her story – because although *you* may think she's going to live to be a hundred, she –

TONY. *That's* changing the subject? It's the same subject!

AVIVA. How is it the same subject? Look, basically I'm talking about knowing who our parents really are as human beings with their own complicated –

TONY. This from someone who left home at sixteen?!

AVIVA. Okay, you're right.

TONY. You know, it's a good thing we didn't get married.

AVIVA. As if that would ever have happened.

TONY. It could have.

AVIVA. No it couldn't.

TONY. At one time?

AVIVA. There's no way that you would ever have married a Jewish girl and you know it. You're a WASH.

TONY. A wash?

AVIVA. A White Anglo Saxon Hebrew. In fact, you've done everything you could to pretend you're not Jewish, from changing your last name…

TONY. For professional reasons.

AVIVA. *(sarcastically)* Oh. Right. I forgot. Tony "Marks." It's not that you're pretending *not* to be Jewish.

TONY. I'm not trying to hide it.

AVIVA. It's simply that there are no actors or singers with Jewish names.

TONY. *(sarcastically)* Who wouldn't *want* to be Jewish?! Haven't you heard we run the banks, the government, labor, *and* industry?

AVIVA. Let me ask you this. Have the two of you ever talked about it privately? What she went through in the camps?

TONY. Did you *see* her leave the room? Just another happy trip down memory lane sitting around and talking about the good old days in the ghetto?

AVIVA. Be serious.

TONY. I am being serious! This was like a fucking nightmare that hung over our house. Plus now? She's just getting over the fact that Dad died.

AVIVA. How has she been dealing with it?

TONY. *(referring to one of the many boxes in the room)* Retail therapy.

AVIVA. *(sighing)* I mean – really.

TONY. My mother's motto is "don't dwell on what's past. We gotta worry about tomorrow." Even when she…

AVIVA. What?

TONY. Never mind.

AVIVA. Even when she…what Tony?

TONY. Look, I'm aware – now – that things were a little different in this house. My parents were immigrants. They spoke Rumanian, Hungarian and Yiddish. We were the family with the funny accents. When you're a kid you just accept it as normal. You try to fit in. You don't know that your parents are meshuga. Then you get married and your wife tells you – in great detail – just how screwed up your family *really* is.

What got you onto this Holocaust thing?

(**AVIVA** *starts searching for something in her bag.*)

AVIVA. A couple years ago I was hired as a guest artist in the high school system. My class was "gang members and the druggies."

TONY. Sounds like a fun job.

AVIVA. Initially, it was – they're so young and raw and beautiful at that age and none of them know it. The only thing they *do* know is that they hate and distrust anyone who is not like them.

But I could relate to their anger, because I was like that as a teenager, too. But I'd found a way to express myself – through my photography – and I *know* that changed my life. So I was really trying to figure out a way to get them excited about life, to get into their heads.

TONY. I bet *they* would have really appreciated the asshole photos.

AVIVA. It's funny you mention that because on the day I was actually going to show them some of my more *recent* stuff, I arrived at school and there spray painted on the door to my classroom, was this HUGE swastika.

TONY. What?!!

AVIVA. I stood there for a moment – I couldn't believe my eyes. So I went in and asked – who did this? Which one of you did this? And of course they were all staring at me, no one speaking and I was shaking so much that I…I mean is that all these kids saw me as? I started scream-ing at them – "Yes, I'm a Jew! I know what this symbol represents! How many of you have ever been picked on, or beaten, or shot at because of your race or religion or ethnic group or sexuality?" Don't you get it? If we can't – oh my god, if we don't start – changing things somehow, getting people to understand that if we keep attacking each other, if we – if we keep *denying* or – I went ballis-tic. I couldn't keep teaching until…Until I learned more myself. About the history. Our history, Tony.

TONY. Where's the completely assimilated Aviva? You never cared about any of this stuff when we were younger.

AVIVA. That's the point. We were younger. And stupider.

TONY. So explain this to me. You've had a religious conversion?

AVIVA. Not exactly.

TONY. Not exactly?

AVIVA. Well, sort of.

TONY. Sort of?

AVIVA. Yes.

TONY. Next you'll be going to synagogue.

AVIVA. Actually I am.

TONY. You're kidding! You're going to synagogue now?!

AVIVA. I'm still Jewish – whether or not I go to synagogue.

TONY. Not according to some Jews.

AVIVA. Look Tony, during the Holocaust it didn't matter *who* you were – you could be religious, you could be an atheist, you could be assimilated – if you were a Jew you were dead. And now to actually have some people say it never happened?

(She hands him the manila envelope and he removes a photo from it.)

This is what I wanted to show you. Did you ever see it?

TONY. Shit. Where did you get that?

AVIVA. I was doing research through the museum and Yad Vashem and there it was. Then I saw your mother's name.

TONY. You have no idea what went on in this house when that photo appeared in the paper.

AVIVA. She's seen it too?

TONY. No. Dad didn't want her to see it. But that didn't keep him from calling Washington and telling them that this was a picture of his wife and the least they could do was give her a name.

AVIVA. Which is exactly what I'm trying to –

TONY. But then she didn't want to leave the apartment because someone might, I don't know. Recognize her.

AVIVA. From that photo? I thought you said she didn't see it.

TONY. She didn't but Dad described it – her and her sister in the work line with the Nazi guard and – I know, it's crazy, but he was always trying to protect her and – listen, if I really understood my mother I'd be in Bellevue.

(**TONY** *takes the photo and hides it in his gym bag.*)

You couldn't find someone else to interview?

AVIVA. I was, but…

TONY. But what?

AVIVA. She died. Last week.

TONY. You interviewed someone and it *killed* her?

AVIVA. I didn't – her name was Ruth Klariche. We met through visual artist's workshop and she also knew your –

(**NAOMI** *reenters carrying a large box filled with papers.*)

NAOMI. Aviva, here –

(*offering box to* **AVIVA**)

TONY. Oh god, Mother!

AVIVA. Mrs. Goldman, I didn't mean to upset you –

NAOMI. I don't know what to do with this. I can't keep, I can't throw away. So. You reminded me. Is this of interest? When you mention, I think somewhere in the bottom of the drawer. Tucked far away.

My husband, sometimes at night he would lock himself in his room. He told me he was writing a book on the war but then he never had a chance to – maybe you could take to Hollywood?

AVIVA. Oh my god. This is a treasure. Tony, don't you want to keep this?

TONY. Why?

NAOMI. You should take.

AVIVA. (*pulling one of the papers out*) This is – this is amazing. Look at how tiny the writing is. I feel funny taking this.

NAOMI. Why? Take. What that man went through…

AVIVA. And what you went through.

NAOMI. Promise me you get it into the right hands?

AVIVA. I promise.

TONY. Great. Now you've got something that you can take back to Mr. Hollywood. Your mission is accomplished. You can go now, huh?

AVIVA. What?

NAOMI. Don't go.

AVIVA. Mrs. Goldman, it was such a pleasure to see you again.

(to **TONY***)*

Zei(t) gezunt! (*Be well – goodbye*)

NAOMI. You know Yiddish?

AVIVA. A bisl. (*Only a little.*) I'm taking a class at Columbia.

NAOMI. You strike me as a very intelligent girl. Why would you want to learn a language no one speaks no more?

AVIVA. That's the same thing my mother said! But my Aunt Esther spoke a little when I was a kid. She had so many great expressions and phrases. She used to say "Yiddish was the luggage of the Jews. That's all we had."

NAOMI. When I was growing, so common, so many people spoke.

AVIVA. I read that eight million people spoke Yiddish at one time. Then a language that existed for over a thousand years disappears? So many killed that an entire *language* vanishes?!

TONY. You know who I feel sorry for? Those ancient Etruscans. Not too many people speaking that language anymore.

AVIVA. Tony, there was a whole literary and cultural identity that resided in Yiddish.

NAOMI. Oh, I'm not smart enough to know anything about that. I only finished seventh grade.

AVIVA. You seem plenty smart to me.

NAOMI. Fun dayn moyl tsu gots oyer.

AVIVA. From your mouth to God's ear.

TONY. From your mouth to God's hearing aid.

AVIVA. I'm trying to become fluent. But it's hard finding anyone to talk with outside of class. I mean, you speak it –

NAOMI. Also Rumanian, Hungarian, Italian. Tony helped to teach me English.

AVIVA. And he did very well.

TONY. Thank you.

AVIVA. Nishto far vos. (*"You're welcome."*)

NAOMI. Good!

AVIVA. It would be great to actually have someone to talk with. Conversationally.

NAOMI. I used to speak Yiddish with my sister all the time.

TONY. Here's some Yiddish for you, Aviva – vos iz di choch-meh? (*"What is the trick?"*)

AVIVA. Chochmeh?!

NAOMI. Vos ret ir epes? (*"What are you talking about?"*)

TONY. I'm listening to you and I'm thinking it's like some rabbi hit you upside the head. A reverse conversion on the road to Damascus.

AVIVA. It's your heritage too.

NAOMI. (*to* **TONY**) Vos ret ir?! (*"What the hell are you talking about?"*) Why must you always push against?

TONY. I'm not buying that someone would be doing this whole Jew fest – if it didn't somehow further their own career. How much money are they giving you? For this project.

AVIVA. I'm going to pretend you didn't just say that. That you weren't stupid enough to –

TONY. Vifl gelt? (*"How much money?"*)

AVIVA. Gelt? This is not about money. You *can* be a real ass-hole, you know that?

TONY. Yeah, I know. You even have the photos to prove it.

NAOMI. A sof! (*"Let's end it!"*)

AVIVA. I'm sorry.

TONY. But she's the one who -!

NAOMI. A SOF!

AVIVA. Really, I'm sorry Mrs. Goldman.

NAOMI. *(referring to the serving tray)* Tony, take these to the kitchen and put away.

TONY. What, so you can talk about me?

NAOMI. I'm your mother, what else do I have to talk about?

> *(**TONY** gathers dishes up. A plate of cookies is left on the table.)*

> Tony? I love you. Ich hob dir lieb. *("I have you love")* Did you hear me?

TONY. *(exiting)* I heard you.

NAOMI. *(to **AVIVA**)* Because if he didn't I have this hearing aid – like new, still in the box –

> *(He is off. Conspiratorially – she's been dying to talk to someone about this.)*

> So did he tell you? Do you know?

AVIVA. What?

NAOMI. He and Elaine…they're separated. Oh, I cry to think about it. You married?

AVIVA. *(caught off guard)* What? No.

NAOMI. No husband?

AVIVA. No.

NAOMI. No children?

AVIVA. No.

NAOMI. And why?

AVIVA. I, uh…I forgot to?

NAOMI. Such a thing you could forget?

AVIVA. Relationships can be tricky.

NAOMI. Yes. With Tony and Elaine I worry, maybe this is my fault. I tell her – if you have bad things to tell me, you tell me to my face, not to my back. Tell me to my face what I'm doing wrong cause I'm not perfect. Nobody is. Ech. Don't get me wrong, I love Elaine, but…

AVIVA. But what?

NAOMI. She is handicapped.

TONY. *(entering)* She is not handicapped! She's Presbyterian!

NAOMI. What difference does it make?

(A phone rings.)

TONY. I'll get it.

*(**TONY** exits down the hallway.)*

NAOMI. But you see – now Tony is - very schpirevdik *("sensitive")* – everything upsets him. The TV is too loud. I shop too much. I breathe too loud. Having Tony staying here is –

AVIVA. Wait. He's actually living here?

NAOMI. *(nodding yes)* He says to make sure I'm all right, that this saves him having to come all the way uptown to check if I'm still breathing. I'm breathing; I'm breathing – much too loud for him.

AVIVA. Mrs. Goldman –

NAOMI. Please, Naomi.

AVIVA. Naomi, what I mentioned earlier, about wanting to talk to you about the war…

NAOMI. Yes, darling? I'm sitting right here.

AVIVA. Could I interview you?

NAOMI. What's there to say? I survived. Why would I want to talk about it?

AVIVA. Because *you* have a *story*. I'd like to hear it.

NAOMI. Oh, I was in bad shape when I came to this country – very sick and all that. And the Doctor put me on my feet, then another Doctor discovered a very good nerve pill that I took twice a day. I don't want for no one to pity me.

AVIVA. What *did* you go through?

NAOMI. What I went through – I became very strong and tough. My doctor says I have a lot of spunk. He tells me he has patients that he has to help in and out of chairs – much younger than I.

AVIVA. It's a very simple process. I'd put you on tape.

NAOMI. Why would I want to be on tape? I can't even watch tapes. Did you see this VCR? Tony bought it for me. I can't figure it out. The time is always blinking twelve, twelve, twelve. Makes me crazy.

(TONY *reenters.*)

TONY. Mother! Did you see a pad of paper with a phone number and some figures on it?

NAOMI. No.

TONY. Elaine's on the phone, she insists that I had it but –

NAOMI. Let me talk to her.

(going to hallway for phone)

TONY. No, I got it. Just…

(TONY *starts after* NAOMI *but she's off. He turns back to* AVIVA.*)*

Stop me if you've heard this one. A judge is interviewing this woman about her pending divorce –

AVIVA. Stop. Your mother told me. You're separated.

TONY. Elaine wants me out of the apartment, but she doesn't want me spending any money on housing – so here I am until the mediator figures out just how many ways nothing can be split.

AVIVA. You might have saved yourself a lot of problems if you'd stuck to Jewish women.

TONY. I *am* stuck with a Jewish woman – problem is she's my mother. All of the work, none of the perks.

AVIVA. Tony, if you'd help me, she'd talk. Giving me these writings from your father? Some part of her wants to but she doesn't know how. Let me start the process and if it gets to be too much –

TONY. What good comes from dwelling on shit like this?

AVIVA. I think that's a question for you and your therapist to discuss.

TONY. I'm not in therapy.

AVIVA. Big surprise.

TONY. Look, if I want to be insulted I'll move back in with my wife.

AVIVA. Can I just explain the process to you?

(pulling out manila envelope again)

The initial interview is this list of questions that I go over with your Mother and the release form – here, look them over. Then I'll come back with a camera man and he'll –

TONY. What?

AVIVA. He runs the camera while I ask her the questions.

TONY. Are you out of your mind?!! You're not bringing anyone else into this apartment. No.

AVIVA. Then I'll run it myself.

TONY. I would never have invited you here in the first place if you'd been up front and told me what this was about.

AVIVA. Don't you think I knew that?

*(**NAOMI** reenters.)*

NAOMI. So am I interrupting?

AVIVA & TONY. No.

TONY. What did you tell Elaine?

NAOMI. I tell her nobody's perfect. Aviva, I've been thinking. About what you asked earlier?

AVIVA. *(hopefully)* Yes?

NAOMI. I would be delighted.

AVIVA. That's terrific!

NAOMI. To teach you Yiddish.

AVIVA. *(switching gears)* Oh. Great!

NAOMI. We can begin our conversation right now.

(Picking up a cookie from the table.)

Di libe iz zis-nor zi iz gut mit broyt. Farshtaist?

AVIVA. Di libe iz zis… "Love is sweet –

NAOMI. – but it's nice to have bread with it."

AVIVA. – nor zi gut mit boyt.

NAOMI. Nishto far vos! (*"very good!"*)

*(**NAOMI** and **AVIVA** continue to speak Yiddish and eat the cookies as **TONY** looks on.)*

(MUSIC/LIGHT SHIFT)

Scene Two

(Later that night. **TONY** *is trying to fix the VCR, looking through an instruction manual.* **NAOMI** *enters with a box of clothes and puts them on the couch to sort. They yell over the sound of static.)*

NAOMI. We could take it back.

TONY. What?

NAOMI. I said we could take it back.

*(***TONY*** turns the sound off.)*

TONY. I don't want to take it back. I want you to be able to watch movies.

NAOMI. Who has time to watch movies?

TONY. You have time to watch the news.

NAOMI. Of course! The world is falling apart; I've got to keep one eye on it.

TONY. You'd use it if it worked, wouldn't you?

NAOMI. If you want me to use it, I'll use it.

TONY. Mother! It's not what I want – it's what you want.

NAOMI. I want what you want.

TONY. Never mind.

NAOMI. What?

TONY. I said NEVER MIND!

NAOMI. You don't have to yell!

TONY. Are you sure you didn't hit a wrong button?

NAOMI. Maybe. Too many buttons.

TONY. *(frustrated with the VCR manual)* God. It'd be nice if someone learned to write these things in English. You didn't enter a password, did ya?

NAOMI. A what?

TONY. Forget it.

NAOMI. I want for you to look at these.

TONY. What are they?

NAOMI. Some clothes of your father's. I found them in the back of the closet, still nice. You should take.

(She pulls out a jacket.)

Here, try this on.

TONY. I don't need a jacket.

NAOMI. Of course you do. Everyone needs a jacket.

TONY. I'm not going to wear that jacket.

NAOMI. It's a good jacket! Your father made this jacket!

TONY. I'm fixing your VCR.

NAOMI. Why do I need a VCR?

TONY. You don't want it? You don't have to have it!

NAOMI. See how good the stitches are? Your father knew how to make.

TONY. Yes – and he worked himself to death doing it.

NAOMI. He provided so that you could have singing lessons, dancing lessons –

TONY. Fat lot of good that did me.

NAOMI. Scha!

TONY. I just didn't think I would be singing at weddings and Holiday Inns.

NAOMI. You sing good! I like to hear you sing. Sing for me.

(No response as he continues to tinker with the VCR.)

Tony, you're alive?

TONY. Yeah, Ma.

NAOMI. You're breathing?

TONY. Yes.

NAOMI. So sing!

*(**TONY** sings some of "Sheyn vi di levone")*

TONY.

DU BIST ARAYN TSU MIR.
IN HARTSN AF KVARTIR.
'KH TRAKHT VI TSU ZOGN DIR
(I'm thinking how to tell you)
AZ DU BIST...
(that you're...)

SHEYN VI DI LEVONE, LIKHTIK VI DI SHTERN
(Beautiful as the moon, Shining like the stars)
FUN HIML A MATONE BISTU MIR TSUGESHIKT.
(As a gift from heaven, you were sent to me)
MAYN GLIK HOB IKH GEVINEN VEN IKH HOB DIKH GEFINEN,
(I gained my happiness when I found you)
SHAYNST VI TOYZNT ZUNEN, HOST MAYN HARTS BAGLIKT
(You shine like a thousand suns, you've gladdened my heart)

DAYNE TSEYNDELEKH, VAYSE PERELEKH,
(Your teeth, white pearls)
MIT DAYNE SHEYNE OYGN,
(With your beautiful eyes)
DAYNE KLEYDELEKH, DAYNE HERELEKH
(Your clothes, your hair)
HOST MIKH TSUGETSOYGN.
(You've captured me)

(He stops.)

You know what? I don't feel much like singing these days, Mom.

NAOMI. Somebody should want such a good jacket. You don't know all that your father went through.

TONY. All I know is that he was gone all day and when he got home he made dinnertime hell. You don't remember any of that?

NAOMI. Your father was a wonderful guy.

TONY. Yeah, sure he was. Why are you so anxious to clear everything out now?

NAOMI. A drive for charity. The rabbi says the other day – oh, I wish he dressed more like a rabbi and less like a slob. Still, he's a good rabbi and he says 'who has to give?' And I do. So –

TONY. It's getting late. I'll put this back and you can do it tomorrow.

*(**TONY** picks box of clothes up.)*

NAOMI. Wait. This I want.

(*She pulls out a handkerchief from the box.*)

For when we light the candle for your father.

(**TONY** *takes the box out and reenters.*)

TONY. Let me get your pills and a little nosh. Do you want the TV on?

NAOMI. Might as well.

(**TONY** *turns on TV and exits to the kitchen.*)

TELEVISION NEWSCASTER. "…Sentencing is expected any day now in the trial of C.I.A. double agent Aldrich Ames. Ames has admitted selling secrets to the Soviet Union and then Russia, in one of the most damaging spy cases in US history. His arrest in February sent shockwaves through the US intelligence community and Mr. Ames admitted to receiving a total of about $2.5 million from the Soviet Union during the nine years he acted as double agent."

(**NAOMI** *smells the handkerchief and holds it. Decides to put the father's jacket into* **TONY**'*s gym bag. Finds photograph.*)

"…today 250,000 Rwandans, mainly Hutus, fled across the border to escape the advancing Tutsi Rwandan Patriotic Front. The U.N. Security council has passed a resolution condemning the killings, but refuses to label these atrocities a genocide. Meanwhile, a person claiming to speak for the Hutu tribe says their real mission, is the extermination of the Tutsis. Scenes of pandemonium were evident everywhere as panicked crowds fought their way through the crowded streets in an attempt to –"

(*The rest of the scene overlaps and builds as* **TONY** *tries to calm her.*)

NAOMI. Tony? Tony?! Tony!!!

TONY. What happened? What's the matter?

NAOMI. Where did this come from?

TONY. Oh, god.

(**TONY** *turns off the TV.*)

NAOMI. Where did this come from?

TONY. I can explain.

NAOMI. Explain? Explain? How can you explain such things?

TONY. Mother, stop.

NAOMI. How does anyone explain such things?

TONY. Stop it! Calm down.

NAOMI. Don't tell me to calm down! This is my sister. This is me.

TONY. It's a mistake that it's here. Let me just put it away. I'm sorry it was –

NAOMI. Jack said – I don't want you should see, you shouldn't see –

TONY. For once he was right!

NAOMI. But I do see it, all the time, I see it here –

(*gesturing to her head*)

– I see it, I see it.

TONY. Here, give me that damn thing.

NAOMI. Don't touch me!

TONY. Ma –

NAOMI. I said don't touch me!!!

TONY. Ma, please –

NAOMI. I don't want to be touched!

TONY. I knew you'd react this way, I knew it –

NAOMI. Everything gone, taken, grabbing all the time. I don't want to be grabbed! No, no, no, no, no, no – my god, Jaaaaaack!!!!

(*MUSIC/LIGHT SHIFT*)

Scene Three

(The next morning. **AVIVA** *is entering from the front door.)*

AVIVA. Hello? Hello!? Mrs. Goldman? Is anybody here?

*(***TONY*** *enters, putting his shirt on. They startle each other.)*

Oh! The door was open.

TONY. The door was open?! She drives me crazy. She can't hear the bell so she leaves the door open.

AVIVA. Isn't your mother expecting me?

TONY. You have no idea what you set off yesterday.

AVIVA. What?

TONY. She found the photo.

AVIVA. Oh my god. But I thought you –

TONY. You don't understand that my mother – the person you want to interview? You've only seen about this much –

(Indicating a small distance with his fingers.)

– of who she really is.

AVIVA. If you mean that she's more complicated than she presents herself –

TONY. Now *there's* an understatement.

(pause)

AVIVA. Have you ever read any of your father's writings?

TONY. Close the fucking box, Pandora!

AVIVA. I was up all night.

TONY. *You* were up all night?!

AVIVA. Tony, your Mother asked me to get this into the right hands and –

TONY. You're like a dybbuk, Aviva, with your nudging and your dredging. At this point you know what I'd like? For this to all go away.

AVIVA. But that's the thing about the past. It doesn't. It can't until –

TONY. *(overlapping)* I *know* you think you're being some kind of Good Samaritan here, Aviva, but you don't know what you're getting into.

AVIVA. I'll take that chance.

(NAOMI, smartly dressed, enters from her bedroom.)

NAOMI. Oh, Aviva! Are you long?

AVIVA. I just got here.

TONY. Ma, did you leave the front door open?

NAOMI. For Aviva.

TONY. We live in New York City!

NAOMI. I know where we live.

(TONY exits to the bedroom to finish getting dressed.)

AVIVA. You look lovely today.

NAOMI. You like? Loehmann's.

(NAOMI returns the photo to AVIVA.)

Aviva. You left this here.

AVIVA. I'm sorry Mrs. Goldman. It wasn't the way that I – I just feel that it's important that –

NAOMI. No. It's past. Done. Now put away.
But you stay for lunch, of course. I will make my special stuffed chicken with the whole skin and the wings.

AVIVA. Sounds delicious.

(TONY reenters.)

NAOMI. I bake it all together with celery, onions and garlic and I bake it for about an hour and a half. Ooohh, the best. For holiday I take it over to Tony and Elaine's, with enough for leftovers. Tony calls me up and says –

TONY. Ma, this chicken is the best chicken I ever ate!

NAOMI. And I say to him, Tony, you full of shit! He say's that to me every time. I learned to cook from my mother, I learned a lot from her. But she died when I was young, so I had no choice but to cook. Vos is di mer mit mir! *("Well, Excuse me!")* What kind of teacher do I make? We should have been saying everything in Yiddish!

(The phone rings. It rings again.)

TONY. Do you want me to – ?

NAOMI. No, no, I *hear* it, I'll get it.

(She exits.)

AVIVA. You know Tony, you were right.

TONY. About?

AVIVA. My interviewing her about the war. It's a bad idea.

TONY. Yes! Thank you – I told you.

AVIVA. I should go.

TONY. No, she'll be very upset if you don't stay for lunch – and it's not just you. Where do I even begin? One minute she's – then the next…it's everything. Dad's death, the nightmares the – ever since I was a kid –

AVIVA. Maybe she'd talk to me about *her* childhood?

TONY. You're relentless!

AVIVA. You always said it was one of my best qualities.

TONY. Aviva, let's drop it now, all right? All right?

(NAOMI reenters from the kitchen.)

NAOMI. Er daf mere. Mr. Jorgenson needs me, his wife. Something's not right.

TONY. Why's he call you?

NAOMI. I try to help people if I can, cause that's how I am. She helped me so much when I got my pacemaker.

AVIVA. You have a pacemaker?

NAOMI. Last year, after Jack died they gave me a pacemaker. The best thing that ever happened to me. I would recommend it for everybody.

(She exits.)

AVIVA. I didn't know she had a pacemaker.

TONY. They call her on the telephone, she has a little machine, they check it out. She takes an aspirin every day. You ever see that old cartoon of a Boy Scout trying to escort a little old lady across the street and she's beating him with her cane because she doesn't think she needs any help? That's my mother.

AVIVA. You remember my Aunt Esther, don't you?

TONY. Sure.

AVIVA. When she had a stroke she developed aphasia… which literally means "not…to speak." Which is why I think it's so important to say things while we still *can*. I would watch Aunt Esther *struggle* to say words, and she'd get so frustrated and I thought, god, there were so many other questions I wanted to ask her but…she was a ziseh neshomeh ("*sweet soul.*")

TONY. You've been studying.

AVIVA. And you can be a sweet soul, too, when you let anyone get close enough. I remember the exact moment I first fell in love with you. I heard you sing in that, god, what was that musical?

TONY. That famous Jewish western musical – *(Yiddish Accent)* Oklahoma.

AVIVA. Right! You were so good.

TONY. Thanks. So – you never married, huh?

AVIVA. No.

TONY. Not that it's any of my business but is there someone?

AVIVA. It's….uh….I'm not sure it's really any of your business.

TONY. Okay. Just curious, that's all.

AVIVA. And you don't have kids?

TONY. They're sticky and spread germs.

AVIVA. Right. So Tony. What's the real reason you're separated?

TONY. Stop me if you've heard this one. This guy Brochstein walks up to Horowitz in the street, taps him on the shoulder and when Horowitz turns, he sends him sprawling to the ground with a solid zetz to the nose. He then says, "Take that, Rosenzweig, you lousy mamzer!!" The bleeding Horowitz shouts back, "I'm Horowitz, you schnook! I am NOT Rosenzweig." Realizing his error, Brochstein apologizes profusely and begs forgiveness for the error of mistaken identity. However, Horowitz remains furious and he screams forth a steady blue stream of epithets. Finally, Brochstein says, "Please Horowitz, calm down. Why are you so upset? Why do you care so much about how I treat Rosenzweig?"

(**AVIVA** *laughs. They kiss. An awkward moment.*)

AVIVA. Wait. You're still –

TONY. Yeah. Elaine says I have issues. That I'm projecting old stuff onto her. There are – things – that I've not come to terms with. All that women's magazine shit.

(**NAOMI** *enters.*)

NAOMI. Tony, Aviva, come. I need your help.

TONY. Why? What happened?

NAOMI. She fell in the shower, blood all over her face. We have to help get her to the hospital.

TONY. I'll get our coats.

NAOMI. Mrs. Jorgenson has that disease where everything flies from your head.

AVIVA. Alzheimers?

NAOMI. Yes. It has been getting worse and worse. But there are times I think that to forget everything would be –

AVIVA. – I've read about it. It sounds so *terrible* –.

NAOMI. *(overlapping)* Terrible? No, no, Aviva. To *forget* – it would be the greatest gift in the world.

(MUSIC/LIGHT SHIFT)

Scene Four

*(Very late that same evening. Open package from QVC sitting on the coffee table, with a piece of clothing laying over the edge. **NAOMI** is asleep in a chair in front of the TV, a late night interview playing. **TONY** enters dressed in his singing clothes. He's a little drunk. He watches his mother for a minute, turns off the TV.)*

NAOMI. They sent the wrong size. If your father was here, he could take it in, make it fit.

TONY. Well, he's not. It's after two…you should get to bed.

NAOMI. I should call her.

TONY. Look, I don't care what you do.

NAOMI. What do you think I should do?

TONY. Don't put this on me.

NAOMI. That look in her eyes.

TONY. Relentless. Like a terrier with a bone.

NAOMI. Mrs. Jorgenson?

TONY. I thought you were talking about – Mrs. Jorgenson has always had a strange look in her eyes. Mrs. Jorgenson was out of her mind before she had a mind to lose.

NAOMI. Last night, again, your father came to me.

TONY. Oh god.

NAOMI. He was crying.

TONY. That's a first.

NAOMI. I say to him, why are you crying? But he just shakes his head. So real. Now I think he is telling me…

TONY. Telling you what?

NAOMI. That it's time. Maybe this would be the right thing.

TONY. What?

NAOMI. She reminds me of someone. Aviva. What should I do?

TONY. Do what you want! Just don't expect me to pick up the pieces again.

NAOMI. I'm not.

TONY. As if I had any choice.

NAOMI. I get along fine. I go. I do.

TONY. Plus now that he's gone it's all up to me, isn't it?

NAOMI. Nothing is up to you.

TONY. You know that's not true!

NAOMI. You don't know the truth.

TONY. Do you think I'm *completely* clueless?

NAOMI. It was very hard for us.

TONY. I know that! But I would hear the two of you whispering late at night and if I walked into the room you'd go silent. Sh! Sh! You made it very clear that it was my job to be *happy* and tell all the cheery stories about what a great family we were and what a wonderful country we now lived in and how none of us had any problems. Wasn't that what you wanted me to say, Mother?

NAOMI. You're drunk.

TONY. Guilty!

NAOMI. I can't tell you what to say.

TONY. But what exactly was I supposed to be, or do or say that would make everything all right?

NAOMI. Tony, I love you.

TONY. Then why don't I *feel* it Mother? You say the words but I feel – every time I think I can pull away, I get sucked back in.

NAOMI. We gave you everything.

TONY. Yes, you did.

NAOMI. Everything we never had.

TONY. I can't make up for what you never had. I'll never be able to make up for what you went through.

NAOMI. You don't know what we went through.

TONY. So fucking tell me then!

(*She slaps him across the face.*)

NAOMI. For *this* I survived the camps?

(**TONY** *exits.* **NAOMI** *starts to go after him but stops. Shocked at her own action she sits down, removes her wig – as if trying to figure out who she really is –and begins to sob.*)
(*MUSIC/LIGHT SHIFT*)

Intermission

Scene Five

(In black. The opening section of the interview.)

AVIVA. Would you please state your full name?

NAOMI. Naomi Goldman.

AVIVA. Could you spell that for me?

NAOMI. N-a-o-m-i G-o-l-d-m-a-n.

AVIVA. And what was your maiden name?

NAOMI. Rosenberg. R-o-s-e-n-b-e-r-g.

AVIVA. Where were you born?

NAOMI. In Nasaud. N-a-s-a-u-d.

AVIVA. Where is that located?

NAOMI. In Rumania, which then became Hungary. It was a nice hometown.

AVIVA. What year were you born?

NAOMI. One-Thousand-Nine-Hundred-and-Twenty-Three.

AVIVA. And the date?

NAOMI. Nineteenth, February.

AVIVA. So when the Nazi's came you were –

*(Lights up. **NAOMI** is sitting in a chair. Without her wig, she is simply yet elegantly dressed. The camcorder is on. **AVIVA** is adjusting a video camera on a tripod. The father's box of writings sits on the coffee table.)*

NAOMI. I was nineteen when they took us to the ghetto in Cluj. It was Friday night. The candles were lit, we were sitting having dinner, and having wine, and the Germans came in, and they pulled down the table cloth and everything fell down and they said "come."

We weren't able to take anything – only the clothes on our back. We never saw our house again.

We lived in the ghetto for about two weeks and then we went to the cattle cars. After we left there – it was very rough for us. We didn't know where we were going.

We were all together. But when we got to Auschwitz they separated us. The men to the left, the women to the right. My father had remarried when my mother died, so now my stepmother…

AVIVA. Yes?

NAOMI. My stepmother was only 42 and she had this little girl – she didn't want to give up her little girl – so they put her in the gas chamber with her child. And my father, too. But we didn't know at the time that our parents were being killed.

AVIVA. How long were you in the camp?

NAOMI. A year in Auschwitz. My mother had been a dressmaker – we always had beautiful dresses. My father had a shoe store – we always had beautiful shoes. The last pair of shoes my father made me I carried in my pocket in the cattle cars when they took us to Auschwitz. I didn't want to give them up they were so beautiful.

Of course they took them away from me.

So after that they took us into a long barracks that we lived on the ground where the rain came in, which is where I got the ear trouble. I had an operation here twice already.

We got there, they took off our clothes, they ripped off our clothes, they threw them away.

They took us to a shower and there was no shower and there was no light. Hundreds of us standing naked and achy.

We were cold.

That's how we were standing there all night until the morning, then there was the light and they gave us permission to take a shower.

AVIVA. Did you know about the other "showers"?

NAOMI. Not at that time. We were just young girls, capable of working, of being put to work. They gave us uniforms; we were all in grey uniforms. They cut our hair – all over. Here, there – all over, they shaved us.

They gave all the same socks and shoes. After awhile my shoes broke and I didn't have shoes, they gave me those duck shoes, those wooden shoes, and I couldn't even walk with them. The clack, clack, clack you know what I mean, you can't walk in them. It was horrible. That's why my husband tells me I can have a thousand shoes when I come to America.

AVIVA. Were you given a number?

NAOMI. Yes. They tattooed me and they told me from now on this is your name. My name was my number. Here. This.

AVIVA. Can you show that to the camera? Thank you. Did you ever see your father and stepmother again?

NAOMI. They put us separate when we arrived. And of course, we were crying for our parents. We were young girls. There was a girl from Nasaud in charge. She was Jewish, but she was a machashayfeh. You know this word?

AVIVA. It means witch.

NAOMI. Yes. She said, "Don't cry, you're going to see your parents on Sunday."

And we said, oh really?

So when Sunday came we didn't see nobody. We asked how? She says, "Look up in the sky – don't you see them? They're all burned up."

AVIVA. That was the first that you knew about the crematoriums?

NAOMI. Yes. But after a while we were put to work, my sisters and I, we worked by the crematorium, separated men's clothes from women's clothes. We saw people go into the ovens. They just put them in the ovens like a bread. And we never saw them again.

AVIVA. Do you need to take a break?

NAOMI. No. Do you?

AVIVA. You're doing very well. Do you know the name Josef Mengele?

NAOMI. Yes.

AVIVA. Did you have any personal contact with him?

NAOMI. My youngest sister Hannah got very, very sick with pneumonia. She was in the hospital and we didn't know about her, and then she was in a different cabin in the compound, and then one day she was back in line for work.

Mengele pulled her out of the work line.

He killed her right in front of us.

He shot her. She was eighteen.

Gillel and I ran over to her, they took a stick and hit us, beat us, then put us back in the line.

AVIVA. Tell me more about your sister.

NAOMI. I know about Hannah as a child growing up, but what kind of person she would have been…I don't know. A good person, I think. I don't know.

It was nothing to take a person and shoot them. Mengele, he was some bastard. He would pull out people for whatever reason, and he shot them.

AVIVA. But you and your other sister continued to work?

NAOMI. We were healthy so we had to go to work. We used to get a pot of soup – and we were in a group and there were about twenty of us in a group and once a day we'd all get a sip out of the same pot.

That was our food.

But when I got sick Gillel, she fed me. My sister was able to go begging for food and she would bring it back and give it to me.

Gillel would dig the part of the grave that I couldn't dig. She was beautiful. And they're all dead now.

AVIVA. So, I'd like to move forward to when the Russians liberated you? And this is 1945?

NAOMI. 27 January. It was in the morning when the Russians opened the doors and, "Come, you're free. The Germans lost. You can go home."

AVIVA. Back to Rumania?

NAOMI. Yes, but we have no money, no clothes, and so at each station we have to wait for the trains to come take us away.

NAOMI. *(cont.)* Once we were at a station waiting for a train and I slept next to a soldier. I moved closer for warmth but in the morning when the train arrived? Everyone got up and this one didn't. He was on the ground dead. But I wasn't afraid. We saw so many in Auschwitz.

AVIVA. But your brother – he survived?

NAOMI. When my sister is waiting at the train this guy comes over, this Hungarian guy – and he asks – What is your name? We say Rosenberg. And he says – I was in the camp with a guy named Rosenberg, a dentist. That's how we found out that our brother was alive and we kept traveling south.

I was so happy to find my brother. When you think all is gone – then to find? My brother wanted to go and kill that machashayfeh because she was liberated and back home. I said, "We are free," and forget about it. Don't you think I'm right?

AVIVA. Yes. And you were traveling home with your sister Gillel and Ruth Klariche?

NAOMI. Who?

AVIVA. Ruth Klariche?

NAOMI. I don't know this woman.

AVIVA. I worked with her on a number of art installations. Ruth told me she knew you.

NAOMI. I never heard of this woman. What did she tell you?

AVIVA. Some soldiers?

NAOMI. There were soldiers everywhere. It was a war.

AVIVA. Yes. Okay. Naomi, part of what I'm also doing is substantiating other testimonies and Ruth said that –

NAOMI. I tell you, I never heard of this woman.

AVIVA. Okay. So…you made your way to a Displaced Persons Camp?

NAOMI. Yes, in Italy.

AVIVA. And that's where you met your husband?

NAOMI. That summer in the DP camp. He said, "I love you, I love you so much, you *need* me and we're going to get married." I said, "You don't even kiss me." And he said, "Oh, can I kiss you? I'm afraid I should insult you."

AVIVA. And then you had Tony?

NAOMI. Jack wanted a family, so…when Tony was born the doctor came over he said "Signora, avete un ragazzo del bambino." But I didn't want…I wanted a girl. That Doctor say to me, "Look Signora, I'll take the boy and you go home and make a girl." But Jack said we were going to keep this baby, what can I say? So I named after the Italian Doctor – Antonio.

AVIVA. You didn't want to name him after a relative?

NAOMI. No. It didn't…it wasn't right.

AVIVA. Do you ever have bad days?

NAOMI. Oh, yes, I have bad days. I remember my family gone, burned, dead. And I see my husband standing by my bed. He was standing by my bed last night, I mean it must have been a dream, I'm not stupid but he opens his mouth to say something…

AVIVA. What?

NAOMI. I don't know cause then I wake up. It was complicated. He took on so much, so much – when other men would have said no.

AVIVA. And what about you? What did you take on?

NAOMI. It's a life. It's my life. That's all. No one should cry for me.

AVIVA. Can we go back to when you were traveling back home – after Auschwitz. You took the train, you walked?

NAOMI. Yes.

AVIVA. Were people helpful? Did they give you food?

NAOMI. Some people gave us food. Some didn't want to see us. Some people said this was all our fault.

AVIVA. Did you witness any acts of violence as you traveled?

NAOMI. There were beatings. There were rapes.

AVIVA. Did you see any of this?

NAOMI. We heard.

AVIVA. You heard but you never saw? Naomi?

NAOMI. What?

AVIVA. I've witnessed what can happen to other survivors when they find the courage to…

NAOMI. To what?

AVIVA. When I spoke with Ruth…

NAOMI. What did Ruth tell you?

AVIVA. She described a farmhouse. Where the three of you hid on your way back to Nasaud.
Why did you ask me back here? Why did you give me your husband's writings?

NAOMI. *(referring to the camera)* Can we turn off?

AVIVA. Of course.

(**AVIVA** *shuts off the camera.*)

Naomi, *why* did you agree to talk to me?

NAOMI. Because…you remind me of my sister. A good person.

AVIVA. So are you. Ruth told me that you saved her life.

NAOMI. I wanted to protect him. To keep him safe. I wanted…

AVIVA. *(overlapping)* It wasn't your fault. None of this was your fault.

NAOMI. On the way back to Nasaud my sister and Ruth and I stopped at a farmhouse. It was deserted. After a while three soldiers came in. We all hid in different places. But they found me…and I said, "I'm all alone." Two of them held me down, and then…they smelled of whiskey…then they take me, one after the other one after the other one after the other…

I was so skinny – like a boy almost – so several months later – I thought no, it can't be. I was not able to think what to do. Even now. Even now.

I saw Ruth once, after. On the street. But I didn't want to see her. You don't want people who knew you then, who knew the things that happened, what you did to… how you…you want to forget. But how can you when… I wanted he should never know. Was it wrong? Maybe that was wrong. If it was your child, would you tell?

AVIVA. Oh, god. Naomi. I…

Afen shpits tsung light di gantse velt.

(**NAOMI** *looks at her.*)

The entire world lies on the tip of the tongue. That's one of the phrases my Aunt Esther taught me – before she wasn't able to speak anymore. Naomi, when we find the words, when we break the silence and tell the truth we can, I don't know, find a way to –

(**TONY** *enters, carrying a VCR box.*)

TONY. So I just went ahead and picked up another VCR since – my god. Wait, wait, wait –

(to AVIVA*)*

How long have you been here?!!

(AVIVA & NAOMI *share a look.)*

AVIVA. I should leave you two alone.

(AVIVA *starts for camera to pack it up.)*

TONY. Where are you going?

AVIVA. I'll stop by tomorrow.

NAOMI. No, sweetheart. Please. Stay. Tony, sit down.

(He sits.)

TONY. Okay Mother, so now what?

NAOMI. Tony, I have a story you should need to know.

(MUSIC/LIGHT SHIFT)

Scene Six

*(After midnight. **AVIVA** has packed her camera equipment. Exhausted, she has fallen asleep on the couch. The box of writings is still on the coffee table. **TONY** enters from the kitchen with coffee.)*

AVIVA. What time is it?

TONY. It's early. Or very late, depending on your point of view.

AVIVA. How are you?

TONY. I'm alive. I'm breathing.

AVIVA. I can see that.

TONY. What was that you said about life taking us to some pretty unexpected places?

AVIVA. Is your mother okay?

TONY. In bed, sound asleep.

AVIVA. I should go, let you get some sleep too.

TONY. I have a lot to think about.

AVIVA. Do you think I'm a terrible person?

TONY. The thought crossed my mind.

AVIVA. I didn't know, honestly, I mean, I hadn't put it all together until –

TONY. I always had this feeling there was another shoe to drop. Who knew it would be *you* who would walk in here one day and throw it at me.

AVIVA. I thought I was doing some good. I wanted to –

TONY. To what? Ambush me?

AVIVA. That wasn't my – I didn't intend –

TONY. *(overlapping)* Not just ambush – this was – I don't know – like being sandblasted, being stripped right down to the…to learn that the reason I'm in this world…was an act of hate? And the whole time she's telling me this, I'm thinking – how – why – would you – what the hell am I supposed to do with this information? Even as there's another part of me that's going – ah, *now* things make sense, *now* things slide into place, *now* things…now –

AVIVA. Now?

TONY. Now I understand. In spite of…he wouldn't hit me. He *tried* to love me in spite of – and how she would be looking at me sometimes – I could never figure it out. I'd think was it something I did? What can I do to… god. Then – then I think about all the shit I put *him* through, how both of us danced around each other all those years, never really…and with my mother – no one being – we were all pretending to be someone else because we were too afraid to…I don't know.

AVIVA. Connect?

TONY. Yeah. Connect.

AVIVA. Remember I told you about that swastika that was painted on my door? After, I was doing some research and I actually looked up the origins of the symbol. It's from Sanskrit meaning – *To be good*. For thousands and thousands of years the swastika represented the wheel of life, sun, moon, good fortune – the union of spirit of the heart of things. Isn't it strange how people can twist something so good into something bad?

*(*AVIVA *goes and gets the interview tape from her bag brings it over to* TONY.*)*

Your father was a remarkable man. He was writing about how people were warned and didn't want to know. People *still* don't want to know.

Here. This tape, I…it's for you and your mom to decide.

(She picks up the camera case to leave.)

TONY. So. Trying to turn something bad into something good?

AVIVA. If it's still possible.

*(*AVIVA *exits.* TONY *moves to the couch, and finally opens the box of his father's writings to see what's inside.)*
(MUSIC/LIGHT SHIFT)

Scene Seven

(**NAOMI** *is sitting alone. She is holding/folding the handkerchief from Scene Two.* **TONY** *enters setting his jacket on the back of a chair.*)

NAOMI. So. A year. Like yesterday.

TONY. This has been the longest year of my life.

NAOMI. Last night –

TONY. Don't tell me. He visited you in your sleep again?

NAOMI. No. Last night I slept for the first time. Like a tree.

TONY. A log.

NAOMI. Okay.

(**TONY** *picks up the interview tape from the table.*)

TONY. What did you decide?

NAOMI. What did *you* decide?

TONY. That it's *your* decision, Mother.

NAOMI. Oscar might give me an award.

TONY. Honestly Mother, if anyone deserves one…

NAOMI. I thought I was doing the right thing.

TONY. I know.

NAOMI. I wanted for you to be free like a bird and fly around. Remember when you were little – I would take you ice skating?

TONY. Yes.

NAOMI. Only I didn't know how to skate so –

TONY. You would hold onto my hand and run all the way around the rink.

NAOMI. I would!

TONY. And I'd be shouting – Coming through! Move aside!

NAOMI. You were such a blabbermouth!

TONY. Rumanian woman on the loose!

NAOMI. And the cold and the snow and the running, I ran – I could run so fast then – I could run and run and run like a young girl.
You were such a beautiful baby.

TONY. We need to get going if we want to make it out to the cemetery before it rains.

(**TONY** *takes the interview tape to put it in his gym bag. He finds the father's jacket* **NAOMI** *placed there. Pulling it out, he takes a moment, decides to put it on. He turns to* **NAOMI.***)*

NAOMI. It's a good jacket.

TONY. Rumanian woman on the loose.

I'll get the cab.

NAOMI. Might as well.

(**TONY** *starts to exit. He leans over to kiss his mother gently on the head and is off.* **NAOMI**, *astonished by his gesture, is swept by emotion. The lights fade.)*

(*MUSIC/LIGHTS*)

End of Play

COSTUMES

NAOMI
1. Fuchsia Skirt
    Matching Striped/Embroidered Sweater
    Cranberry Shoes
    Cranberry Purse
    Silk Tweed Coat
    Floral Silk Scarf
    Gold Chain
    Multi-colored Crystal Earrings
    (Underdressed #2 costume)

2. B/W/Gold Print knit Dress
            W/ Attached Red Bead Necklace
    Black Shoes
    Wig

3. B/W Striped Knit Top
    Matching Black Knit Skirt with Ruffle Hem (A)
    Darker Colored Crystal Earrings
    Rose Pin
    Repeat Black Shoes

4. Blue Robe w/ Sash
    Blue Slippers

Act Break

5. Cranberry/Tan/Black Floral Print Blouse
    A-Line Flare Black Knit Skirt (B)
    Repeat Black Shoes
    Mic pack waist belt

6. Seafoam Green 2 pc Boucle Suit
    White Embroidered Blouse
    Bone-Colored Shoes
    Large Multi-Pearl Earrings w/ matching
    Pearl Necklace w/ matching
    Pearl and Rhinestone Pin (on suit lapel)

AVIVA
1. Brown "moleskin" coat
    Logan Green Skirt
    Maroon Zippered Knit Cardigan
    Magen David (Jewish Star) on Gold Chain
    Light Green V-Necked Tank Top
    Amber bead necklace
    Amber Earrings
    Brown Satchel
    Med Brown Shoes w/ Princess Heel

2. Blue Knit Top
   Blue/Tan/Brown Print Challis Shirt
   Blue Bead Necklace w/ Matching Earrings
   Repeat Jewish Star Necklace
   Repeat Med Brown Shoes

Act Break

3. Brown Knit Pants
   Green Ribbon Knit Top
   Dark Brown Faux Lizard Shoes w/ Chunky Heels
   Repeat Magen David Necklace (no other necklace)
   Repeat amber earrings

TONY

1. Blue Patterned Shirt
   Navy Blue T-shirt
   Khaki Pants
   Dark Socks
   Brown Shoes
   Brown Belt
   Windbreaker

2. Repeat

3. Repeat Khakis/belt/shoes etc
   White V-Necked T-Shirt
   Orange Shirt

4. Tux Jacket and Pants
   Rigged Tux Shirt/Vest Tie Combo
   Black Shoes

Act Break

5. Repeat Khakis/belt/shoes etc
   Light Blue T-shirt
   Repeat Windbreaker

6. Repeat T-Shirt/Pants

7. Repeat Shoes
   Add Red/Blue Glen Plaid Shirt w/ Rigged Tie Combo

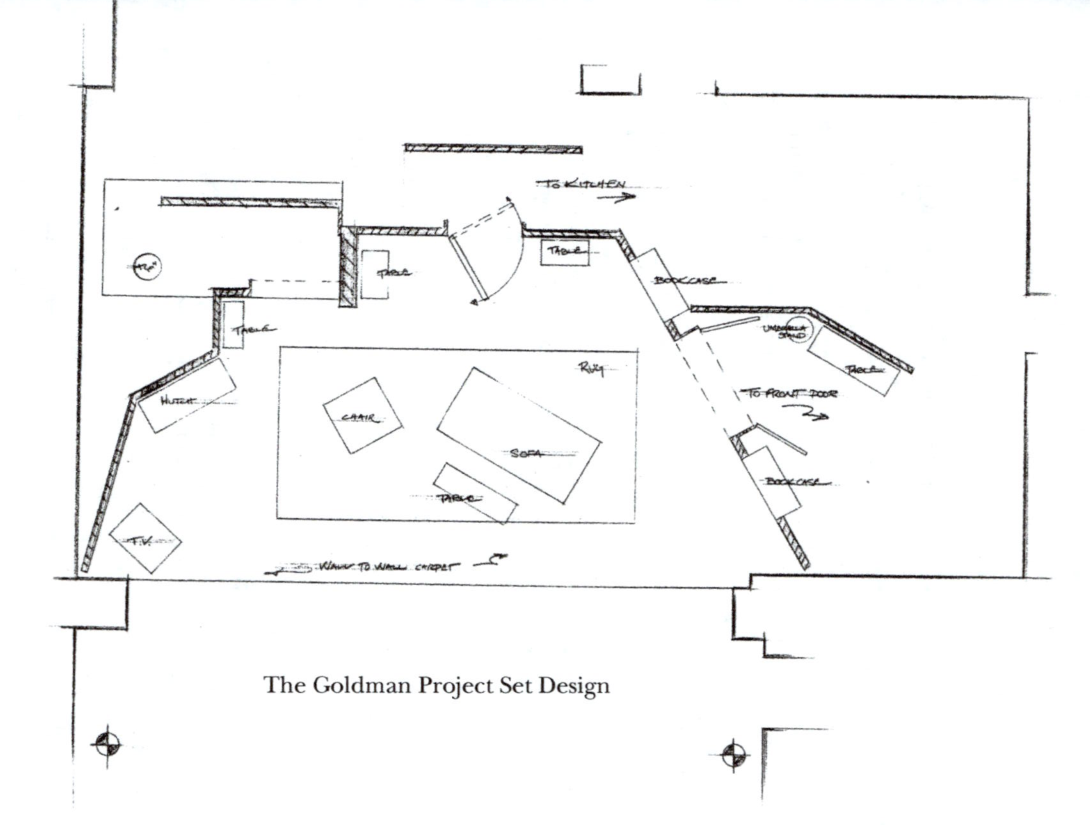

The Goldman Project Set Design

From the Reviews of
THE GOLDMAN PROJECT...

"Introducing Naomi, a Romanian-born widow, as a lovably comic, more than a little stereotypical character...a smart decision on the part of Staci Swedeen"
- Anita Gates, *The New York Times*

"Swedeen has an ear for dialogue, even the passages in Yiddish fit the moment nicely. (Don't worry: The Yiddish is instantly translated in the course of the conversation.)"
- Peter D. Kramer, *The Journal News*

"This fine play is less about the past than about living with honesty in the present."
- James F.Cotter, *Times Herald-Record*

"The play is intelligently and sensitively written...The author is concerned with the Holocaust itself but also the residue it has left not only on those who suffered but on family members."
- Wolf Entertainment

"Each of these characters is shrouded in a bit of mystery, and Ms. Swedeen coyly raises questions about their motivations that give the first act an appealing ambiguity."
- Jason Zinoman, *The New York Times*

"Rarely have I been so riveted by exceptionally thought-provoking and subliminally disturbing theatre as I was, while attending *The Goldman Project*, by Staci Swedeen."
- Roberta on the Arts

"Swedeen's script seemed to come to life in all three of the performances as the play moved toward its conclusion. She should be commended for taking a very difficult and shattering subject, peppering it with humor and humanity, leaving the audience satisfied that they've seen an admirable evening of theatre."
- TheaterScene.net

"The further the world spins away from World War II, the more deconstructed, alienated and "artistic" Holocaust-related plays have become. This is not the case with *The Goldman Project*, which realistically captures the confrontational dynamic of a survivor parent and second generation (adult) child. "
- Masha Leon, *The Forward*

www.ingramcontent.com/pod-product-compliance
Lightning Source LLC
Chambersburg PA
CBHW070419120726
47909CB00005B/1710

* 9 7 8 0 5 7 3 6 7 0 3 9 8 *